THIS BOOK BELONGS TO

_____

_____

First published in hardback in Great Britain by HarperCollins Children's Books in 2009
First published in paperback in 2010

3 5 7 9 10 8 6 4

ISBN: 978-0-00-735159-6

HarperCollins Children's Books is a division of HarperCollins Publishers Ltd.

Text and illustrations copyright © Emma Chichester Clark 2009

Text abridged by Alison Sage and retold by Emma Chichester Clark

Visit our website at www.harpercollins.co.uk

Printed in China

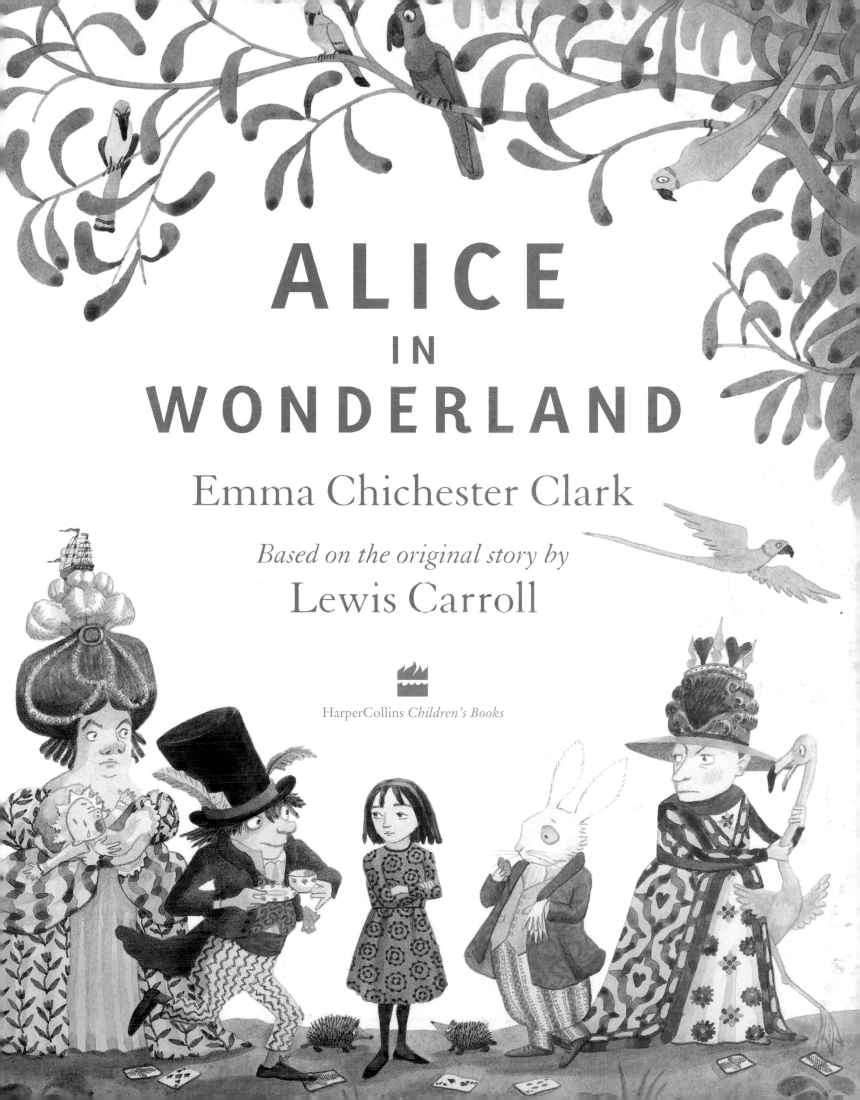

ALICE
IN
WONDERLAND

Emma Chichester Clark

Based on the original story by

Lewis Carroll

HarperCollins *Children's Books*

Alice was sitting with her sister on the riverbank. She'd never felt so bored. There was nothing to do. She'd half-thought of making a daisy chain, but couldn't be bothered to get up and pick the daisies. Her sister's book looked duller than dull. "What's the use of a book," thought Alice, "without pictures or conversation?"

But at that moment a white rabbit with pink eyes and a jacket to match rushed by. "Oh, dear! Oh, dear! I'll be late!" he said as he looked at his pocket watch.

Alice leapt up and ran after him, just as he disappeared down a rabbit hole. Suddenly she was falling…

   falling…

    and falling…

Down…

down…

down…

she fell, quite slowly, looking at shelves all around her as she went. She seemed to be falling forever and was just wondering if she was anywhere near the centre of the earth, when she landed – thump! – on a pile of dry leaves.

The White Rabbit rushed ahead down a long, dark passage. "Oh, my ears and whiskers!" he muttered. "How late it's getting."

Alice raced after him, but he completely vanished, and she found herself alone in a long hall with doors on either side. Every door was locked. How was she to get out again?

Eventually Alice noticed a glass table with a little golden

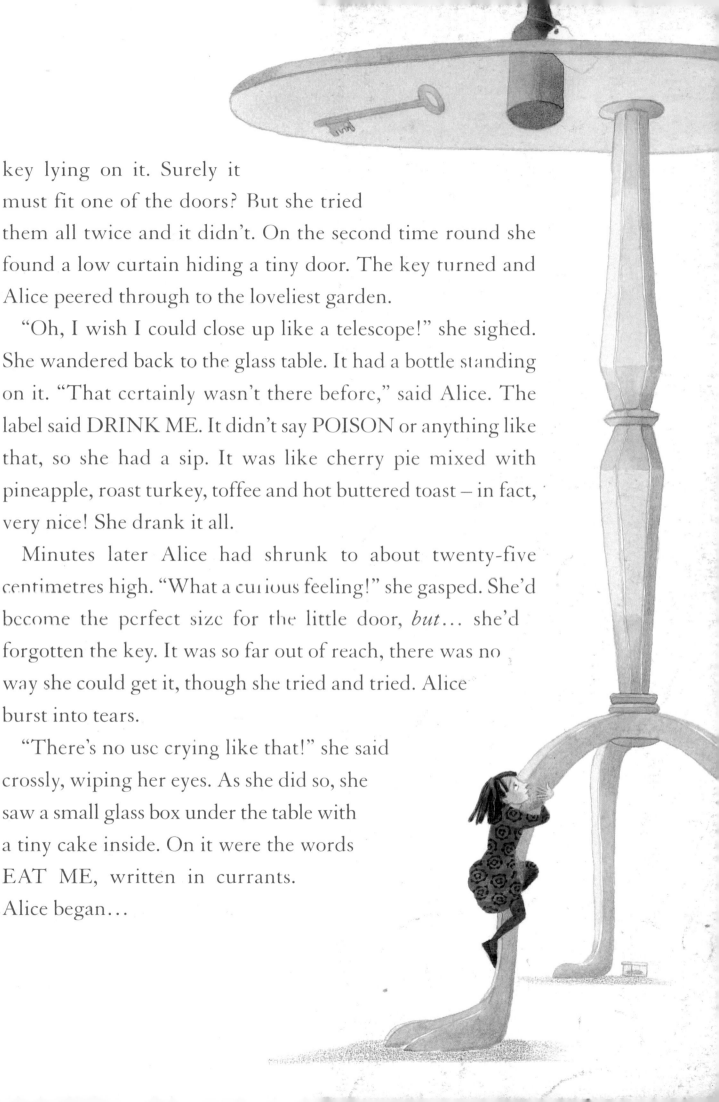

key lying on it. Surely it
must fit one of the doors? But she tried
them all twice and it didn't. On the second time round she
found a low curtain hiding a tiny door. The key turned and
Alice peered through to the loveliest garden.

"Oh, I wish I could close up like a telescope!" she sighed.
She wandered back to the glass table. It had a bottle standing
on it. "That certainly wasn't there before," said Alice. The
label said DRINK ME. It didn't say POISON or anything like
that, so she had a sip. It was like cherry pie mixed with
pineapple, roast turkey, toffee and hot buttered toast – in fact,
very nice! She drank it all.

Minutes later Alice had shrunk to about twenty-five
centimetres high. "What a curious feeling!" she gasped. She'd
become the perfect size for the little door, *but*... she'd
forgotten the key. It was so far out of reach, there was no
way she could get it, though she tried and tried. Alice
burst into tears.

"There's no use crying like that!" she said
crossly, wiping her eyes. As she did so, she
saw a small glass box under the table with
a tiny cake inside. On it were the words
EAT ME, written in currants.
Alice began...

"Curiouser and curiouser! Goodbye, feet!" cried Alice. She was growing… taller and taller. When her head hit the ceiling, she knew it was hopeless to even think of the lovely garden and that made her cry again. She felt so desperate that when the White Rabbit appeared, she hoped he'd help, but he shrieked with horror, dropping his fan and gloves, and ran away.

Poor Alice. Everything was so peculiar that she wasn't even sure who she was any more. Everything was scrambled and upside down.

Suddenly she realised she'd put on one of the little gloves. "How could I have done that?" she wondered. "I must be growing small again." And she ran to the garden door. But it was locked, the key on the table, as before.

"Things are worse than ever!" cried Alice. But then, worse than that, she slipped and was immediately up to her chin in water, swimming in a pool of her own tears. Several other creatures were splashing about too. Among them were a mouse, a duck, a dodo, an eaglet and a lory. It was quite crowded.

"I wish I hadn't cried so much," sniffed Alice.

Alice led the party to the shore. They were all cross and dripping.

"The best thing to get us dry would be a Caucus race," said the Dodo. He paused and waited for someone to speak.

"What is a Caucus race?" asked Alice obligingly.

"The best way to explain it is to do it," said the Dodo. He marked out a racecourse in a sort of circle. All of them stood inside it. There was no, "One, two, three, GO!" Everyone ran when they liked and stopped when they liked, so it was hard to know when it ended, but after about half an hour, when everyone was dry, the Dodo called out, "The race is over!"

"Who's the winner?" they all asked.

"Everybody has won, and all must have prizes!" replied the Dodo, looking at Alice, who had no idea what to do. She found some sweets in her pocket and handed them out. There was a lot

of complaining – some saying that they didn't taste of anything. But after they'd all been eaten, the Mouse began to speak.

"Mine is a long and sad tale…"

"It certainly is a long tail," said Alice. "But why sad?"

"You're not listening properly!" snapped the Mouse and he stomped off.

"Come back!" cried the others, but he just walked faster.

"I wish Dinah was here," said Alice to nobody in particular. "She'd soon get him back."

"Who's Dinah?" asked the Lory.

"Oh, Dinah's my cat," said Alice fondly. "She's so good at catching mice and birds…" Alice stopped. She was suddenly alone once more. At the mention of dear Dinah, they'd all hurried away.

"Oh, my dear Dinah!" sighed Alice. "I wonder if I'll ever see you any more!" This thought, and being so lost and alone, made Alice cry all over again, until hearing the pattering of footsteps, she looked up and saw the White Rabbit, anxiously searching for something.

"Mary Ann!" he said crossly when he noticed Alice. "What are you doing out here? Run home and fetch me my fan and gloves! Quick now!"

Alice was so shocked at being ordered about by a rabbit, she ran off in the direction he pointed. "He must have thought I was his maid," she guessed. "I suppose Dinah'll be ordering me about next!"

Alice arrived at a little house with W. RABBIT on the door and ran upstairs to the bedroom where, as well as the gloves and fan, there was a bottle on the mantelpiece. "Something interesting is sure to happen," she said to herself as she put it to her lips. "I hope it'll make me taller again. I'm so tired of being such a tiny little thing." She put her hand on top of her head to see which way it was growing. Sure enough, sooner than she'd hoped, she had grown so large she couldn't possibly move or get out of the room. She had to fold herself up, dangling one arm out of the window and one foot up the chimney. It was very uncomfortable and Alice felt extremely unhappy.

"Mary Ann!" cried the White Rabbit. "Fetch me my gloves at once!" He was trying to open the door but Alice's other elbow was pressed against it.

Alice forgot that she was about a thousand times bigger than the Rabbit and began to shake with fright which made the whole house tremble.

"I'll go round and get in the window," Alice heard the Rabbit say.

"That you won't!" she thought. She spread out the hand that was outside and snatched in the air.

There was a shriek and a crash, then the Rabbit's angry voice, "Pat! Pat! See that arm in the window? It's got no business there! Take it away!"

"Sure, I don't like it, yer honour, at all, at all!" said another voice.

Alice didn't like it at all either. She wished they could pull her out of the window. But the plan was to send Bill down the chimney – whoever Bill was. Alice drew her foot back and when she heard scrabbling sounds, she gave a sharp kick.

"There goes Bill!" cried the Rabbit. "Well, we'll burn the house down!" he said.

"If you do," shouted Alice, "I'll set Dinah on you!" That silenced them.

A minute later she heard the Rabbit say, "A barrowful will do it!" and suddenly a shower of pebbles came rattling through the window.

"Stop it at once!" cried Alice, but as she watched, the pebbles were turning into little cakes all over the floor. She ate one and immediately began shrinking. When she was small enough, she ran down the stairs and away as fast as she could. There was a little group crowded around a half-conscious lizard. "I suppose that's Bill," thought Alice.

On the far side of a thick wood Alice stopped to catch her breath. "The first thing I've got to do," she said, "is grow to my right size again. I guess I'd better eat or drink something, but the question is, what?"

In front of her was a large mushroom. As she peeped over the edge, her eyes met those of a big blue caterpillar.

"Who are you?" it asked.

"I… I hardly know, sir, just now," Alice began. "At least, I know who I was when I got up this morning, but I think I must have changed several times since then."

The Caterpillar was not at all sympathetic. It just repeated the question, "Who are you?"

Alice began to feel irritated. "I think you ought to tell me who *you* are first," she said.

"Why?" asked the Caterpillar. He seemed so grumpy, Alice began to walk away.

"Come back!" said the Caterpillar. "I've something important to say!"

Alice stopped.

"Keep your temper!" he said.

"Is that all?" said Alice angrily.

"What size do you want to be?" asked the Caterpillar.

"Well, I would like to be a little larger, if you wouldn't mind," she replied. "Eight centimetres is such a wretched height."

"It is a very good height indeed!" the Caterpillar snapped. Then he yawned twice, slid down from the mushroom and began to crawl away, muttering as he went, "One side will make you taller; the other, shorter."

"One side of what?" thought Alice.

"Of the mushroom," said the Caterpillar, just as though she had spoken aloud.

Alice stretched round it and broke off a piece in each hand. "Which is which?" she wondered.

With a few adjustments, nibbling first one piece, then the other, Alice arrived at twenty-three centimetres in time to see two footmen (well, they *looked* like footmen, in uniform – except they were a frog and a fish) running towards a little house. As they met, they bowed so low that their wigs became tangled up.

The Fish Footman held a big envelope. "For the Duchess," he said. "An invitation from the Queen to play croquet!"

There were dreadful noises coming from the house – howling, sneezing and the smashing of plates.

The Frog Footman was rather unhelpful when Alice approached him. He just sat and stared vacantly at the sky.

"I shall sit here," he sighed, "till tomorrow…"

Suddenly the door opened and a plate flew straight at his head. Alice rushed in and found herself in a kitchen full of smoke and the smell of hot pepper.

The Duchess sat nursing a baby, while the cook stirred a huge pot of smoky soup. Everyone, except for a large cat, was sneezing. The cat grinned from ear to ear.

"Can you tell me," Alice began as politely as she could, "why your cat is grinning like that?"

"Because it's a Cheshire Cat," said the Duchess. "Pig!"

Alice jumped, but then realised the Duchess meant the baby, who was shrieking.

"I didn't know cats could grin," said Alice.

"You don't know much, and that's a fact!" said the Duchess.

A moment later the cook began to throw everything in sight at the Duchess and the baby – saucepans, plates and bowls showered over them.

"Oh! Watch out!" cried Alice. "His precious nose!"

"If everybody minded their own business, the world would go round a great deal faster than it does!" growled the Duchess.

She began singing a sort of lullaby, throwing the baby over her head at the end of each line. It screamed louder than ever. Then, flinging it in Alice's direction, the Duchess said, "You have it! I'm off to play croquet with the Queen!" A frying pan just missed her as she went.

The baby was wriggling and snorting like a steam engine. Alice managed to hold it by twisting it up into a kind of knot, seizing an ear and a foot. Now it had begun to grunt and, in daylight, seemed to look more and more pig-like. Its nose was definitely a snout and its eyes were too small. In fact, Alice didn't like the look of it at all and suddenly felt silly carrying it around, so she put it down and watched it trot away into the trees. "If it had grown up," she said to herself, "it would have made a dreadfully ugly child, but it makes a rather handsome pig."

It was then that Alice realised the Cheshire Cat was watching her from a tree, grinning as ever, displaying magnificent claws and teeth.

"Could you tell me, please, which way to go from here?" asked Alice.

"That depends on where you want to get to," said the Cat.

"I don't particularly care where..." said Alice.

"Then it doesn't matter which way you go," said the Cat. "That direction lives a Hatter," he waved a paw, "and that direction, a March Hare. Visit whichever you like – they're both mad. Are you playing croquet with the Queen today?"

"I'd like to, but I haven't been invited," answered Alice.

"You'll see me there," said the Cat and vanished. Then he suddenly reappeared. "Oh, by the way, what happened to the baby?"

"It turned into a pig," replied Alice quietly.

"I thought it would," said the Cat, before disappearing again. Then suddenly he was back. "Did you say 'pig' or 'fig'?"

"I said 'pig'," answered Alice.

This time the Cat faded away slowly, leaving only its grin behind.

When Alice saw the March Hare's house with its chimneys shaped like ears, she quickly ate a little more mushroom to make herself taller. Under a tree was a long table where the March Hare and the Hatter were sitting at one end, having tea. They were resting their elbows on a dormouse that was fast asleep.

"No room! No room!" they cried as they saw Alice coming.

"There's plenty of room!" said Alice indignantly, and she sat down in an armchair.

The Hatter stared at her. "Your hair needs cutting!" he said.

"You shouldn't make personal remarks," said Alice. "It's rude."

The Hatter's eyes opened even wider. "What's the difference between a raven and a writing desk?" he asked as he took out his watch and held it to his ear. "And what's the date today?"

"The fourth," said Alice.

"Bother! Two days wrong. I knew butter wouldn't fix it!"

"It was the best butter," the Hare said quietly.

"But it had crumbs in it," moaned the Hatter.

The Hare reached for the watch and dipped it in his tea.

"The Dormouse is asleep again," said the Hatter, pouring a little tea on its nose.

"Of course… of course…" murmured the Dormouse.

"Can you answer the riddle yet?" the Hatter asked Alice.

"No," replied Alice wearily. "I give up. What is the answer?"

"I haven't the slightest idea," said the Hatter.

"Twinkle, twinkle, little bat!" the Hatter was singing. *"How I wonder what you're at!"* he continued. "Do you know it?" he asked.

"I've heard something like it," said Alice.

"It goes on: *Up above the world you fly, like a tea tray in the sky.* When I sang it to the Queen, she threatened to cut my head off," he said sadly. "She said I wasn't keeping time, and it's true: time never works for me, so now we let it stay at six o'clock."

"So it's always tea time?" asked Alice brightly.

"Yes," sighed the Hatter. "And no time for washing-up."

"So you keep moving round the places," Alice guessed.

"Exactly," said the Hatter.

"But what happens when you get to the beginning again?" asked Alice.

The March Hare yawned. "Let's change the subject. I vote the young lady tells us a story."

"I'm afraid I don't know any," said Alice.

"Then the Dormouse will!" the Hare and the Hatter cried, pinching him fiercely.

The Dormouse gasped, "There were three little sisters who lived in a well…"

"What did they eat?" asked Alice.

"Treacle," replied the Dormouse. "And they were very ill. They were learning to draw everything that begins with 'M'…"

"But why 'M'?" asked Alice.

"Why not?" said the March Hare.

"Time to move round!" announced the Hatter.

"They drew mousetraps and the moon," the Dormouse continued, "and memory and muchness – you know how you say things are much of a muchness – have you seen a drawing of a muchness?"

"Um," began Alice, more confused than ever. "I don't think…"

"Then you shouldn't speak!" snarled the Hatter.

That was enough for Alice. She got up and walked away. Nobody seemed to notice or care, as she'd half-hoped they would. The last thing she saw was the Hatter and the March Hare trying to stuff the Dormouse into the teapot.

"That was the stupidest party I've ever been to," she said to herself. Just as she said it, she noticed a little door in one of the trees. "That's very curious," she thought, "but everything's curious today." And in she went.

Once more Alice found herself in the long hall, close to the glass table. First she picked up the key and unlocked the door to the garden. She was determined to get it right this time. Then she nibbled at the piece of mushroom she'd saved, until she became just small enough.

At long last she walked down the passage and through the door, into the beautiful garden, full of bright flower beds and cool fountains.

A rose tree with white roses stood near the entrance. Three gardeners were busy painting the roses red at great speed.

"Would you tell me," said Alice, "why you are doing that?"

They all looked terrified, but one of them explained, "We were meant to plant red ones… If the Queen finds out, she'll cut off our heads!" Then all three threw themselves to the ground, face down, as a magnificent procession approached. Alice wasn't sure if she was meant to lie down beside them, but decided not to.

"Who is this?" the Queen of Hearts roared.

"My name is Alice, your Majesty," Alice said politely. But she thought, "They're only a pack of cards! Nothing to be scared of!"

"And who are these?" The Queen pointed at the gardeners.

"How should I know?" Alice answered.

The Queen went bright red with anger and screamed, "Off with her head!"

"Nonsense!" said Alice, and the Queen was silent, until she saw what the gardeners had done.

"Off with their heads!" she cried. Then the procession moved on.

"You won't be beheaded," Alice assured the gardeners. She quickly hid them in a flowerpot and followed the Queen.

"Get to your places!" the Queen bellowed with a voice like thunder, and people began running about in all directions.

Alice thought she'd never seen such a peculiar croquet pitch in her whole life.

The pitch was covered in lumps and bumps, and the hoops were soldiers bent double. Now and then they wandered off, as did the hedgehogs that were meant to be balls. The mallets were live flamingos, which were impossible to aim properly. Every time Alice tried, hers would twist itself round and look at her oddly, which made Alice giggle.

The players all played when they liked, and the Queen, in a furious rage, was stomping about, yelling, "Off with their heads!"

Alice felt extremely nervous, but to her relief, the Cheshire Cat appeared. "Now I've got someone to talk to," she thought.

But when the King suggested it kiss his hand, the Cat said, "I'd rather not!" which set the Queen off again.

"Off with his head!" she screeched. (Only his head was visible, so nobody knew how this could be done.)

Alice was astonished when the Duchess took her arm and said, "I *am* glad to see you again, you dear old thing!"

But then the Queen roared, "Either you or your head must be off!" and the Duchess rushed away. The Queen turned to Alice, "Have you seen the Mock Turtle yet?"

"No," said Alice. "I don't even know what a Mock Turtle is."

"It's the thing Mock Turtle soup's made from," said the Queen. "He'll tell you his story. Come on!"

But first they met a Gryphon, lying asleep in the sun.

"Up you get, you lazy thing, and take this girl to meet the Mock Turtle," ordered the Queen.

"What fun!" said the Gryphon as it rubbed its eyes.

"Why fun?" asked Alice.

"Oh, *her*. It's all her fantasy, you know. They never do execute anyone," laughed the Gryphon. "Come on!"

"I've never been so bossed about," thought Alice.

Far along the beach they met the Mock Turtle sitting sad and lonely, on a little ledge of rock. His eyes were full of tears and, between sobs, he told his story. "We went to school in the sea.

Our teacher was a turtle, but we called him 'Tortoise'…"

"Why 'Tortoise'?" asked Alice.

"Because he taught us!" snapped the Mock Turtle. "We learnt Reeling and Writhing, Ambition, Distraction, Uglification and Derision… and Mystery."

"Wow!" said Alice. "How many hours a day were your lessons?"

"Ten hours the first day, nine the next, and so on," said the Mock Turtle.

"That's why they're called 'lessons'," explained the Gryphon. "They lessen each day."

"As you've never lived below sea," went on the Mock Turtle, "you can't know how brilliant a Lobster Quadrille is."

Alice shook her head.

"Make two lines!" cried the Mock Turtle. "Seals, turtles, salmon and so on. Clear away the jellyfish…"

"And you throw all the lobsters," the Gryphon leapt as he spoke, "far out to sea!"

The Mock Turtle was skipping about. "Swim after them and do a somersault," he shrieked.

"Then swap lobsters!" yelled the Gryphon.

"And back to land," groaned the Mock Turtle, and both creatures slumped on the sand, looking at Alice sadly.

"Nice…" said Alice quietly.

"Let's do it!" the creatures cried and leapt up again. They danced round Alice in a figure of eight, while the Mock Turtle sang a gloomy song about a fish called a whiting.

"I s'pose you've seen a whiting?" asked the Mock Turtle.

"Oh yes!" said Alice. "At dinn…" She stopped herself quickly.

"I don't know where Dinn is, but you know what they're like," said the Mock Turtle. "Good for cleaning white shoes."

"Now let's hear some of your adventures," the Gryphon said to Alice.

Alice wasn't sure how to begin. "Well," she said. "There's no point in thinking of yesterday, because I was someone else then…"

It was alarming the way the creatures kept moving in, closer and closer, opening their mouths very wide, but finally, after many attempts at reciting various poems, the Mock Turtle remembered his favourite, which he began in a voice choked with sobs:

"Beautiful Soup, so rich and green,
Waiting in a hot tureen!
Who for such dainties would not stoop?
Soup of the evening, beautiful Soup!
Soup of the evening, beautiful Soup!
Beau-ootiful Soo-oop!
Beautiful Soo-oop!
Soo-oop of the e-e-evening,
Beautiful, beautiful Soup!"

The Mock Turtle was about to go on, when they heard a cry in the distance, "The trial's beginning!"

"Come on!" cried the Gryphon as he grabbed Alice's hand.

They ran until they came to the courtroom, where the King and Queen of Hearts, and a great crowd of birds and animals, and the whole pack of cards were waiting. The King was the Judge. The Knave stood before him, in chains, and the twelve jurors were busy writing their names on slates. Bill, the Lizard, had a squeaky pencil, which Alice couldn't stand, so she took it from him and he went on writing with his finger.

Alice gazed at the huge plate of tarts in the middle of the room.

Then the White Rabbit blew his trumpet. "Silence in court!" he cried before reading from a scroll:

"The Queen of Hearts, she made some tarts,
All on a summer day:
The Knave of Hearts, he stole those tarts,
And took them quite away!"

"Call the first witness!" said the King to the White Rabbit.

"First witness!" called the Rabbit.

This was the Mad Hatter. He held a cup of tea in one hand and a piece of bread and butter in the other.

"Take off your hat!" said the King.

"It isn't mine!" replied the Hatter nervously.

"*Stolen!*" exclaimed the King. The jury began writing notes furiously.

"No! No! I sell them!" said the Hatter, shaking with fright. "I'm a hatter." Then he took a large bite out of his teacup instead of the bread and butter.

When the Hatter mentioned the March Hare in his evidence, the Hare denied everything vigorously, and the King eventually told him to stand down.

"And just take off his head outside," said the Queen to the officers, but the Hatter was already out of sight.

Alice, meanwhile, had suddenly started growing.

"Stop squeezing!" complained the Dormouse. "You've got no right to grow in *here!*"

The next witness was the Duchess's cook. She was holding a pepper pot and everyone began sneezing.

"Give your evidence!" demanded the King.

"Shan't!" replied the cook.

The King looked anxiously at the White Rabbit, who hissed, "Go on!"

"What are the tarts made of?" the King continued.

"Pepper," said the cook.

"Treacle," said the Dormouse sleepily.

"Off with his whiskers!" shrieked the Queen.

For some minutes the whole courtroom was in confusion.

"Never mind!" said the King. "Call the next witness!"

The White Rabbit looked at his list, then he called out, "Alice!"

Alice jumped up, forgetting how large she'd grown, and tipped over the jury box.

"Oh! I'm so sorry," she said, and began to put them all back in their places. She put Bill in upside down by mistake, and turned him the right way up again. "Not that he'll be any more useful," she thought.

"Silence! Rule Forty-two!" the King shouted, staring at Alice. "All those more than a kilometre high must leave court!"

"I'm not a kilometre high," said Alice.

"Nearly two kilometres high!" said the Queen, throwing an ink pot at Bill.

"Let the jury consider their verdict!" said the King.

"No! No! Sentence first, verdict after!" cried the Queen.

"Rubbish!" said Alice. "That's not how it works."

"Hold your tongue!" said the Queen, turning purple.

"I won't!" said Alice.

"Off with her head!" yelled the Queen at the top of her voice.

"Whatever!" said Alice. "I'm not scared of you! You're just a pack of cards!"

At that, the whole pack rose up in the air like a tornado, and came flying down on Alice. She tried to beat them off, half-laughing, half-crying…

"Alice! Alice, wake up!"

Alice opened her eyes to find her sister gently brushing fallen leaves from her face.

"Oh, I've had such a strange dream," she said, and she told her sister all about it.

When she'd finished, her sister hugged her. "It sounds incredible… amazing!" she said. "But now you must go, or you'll be late for your tea."

So Alice jumped up and ran as fast as she could, thinking as she ran, over and over, of all the extraordinary things that had happened to her; the White Rabbit, the Hatter, the Duchess, the Caterpillar, the Queen of Hearts… So many creatures… so many things! What a wonderful dream it had been!